MEINRAD INGLIN

FOUR STORIES

Published in paperback in 2023 by Sixth Element Publishing
on behalf of the Meinrad Inglin Foundation, Switzerland

Sixth Element Publishing
Arthur Robinson House
13-14 The Green
Billingham TS23 1EU
www.6epublishing.net

ISBN 978-1-914170-47-8

British Library Cataloguing in Publication Data. A catalogue record for
this book is available from the British Library.

Printed in Great Britain.

MEINRAD INGLIN

FOUR STORIES

TRANSLATED BY
CHRIS WALTON

This publication was kindly funded by the Meinrad Inglin Foundation (www.meinradinglin.ch). The translator is grateful to Kate Hopkins for valuable advice in the final stages of this book.

The cover image is a still from the animated film Greylands by Charlotte Walter and Alvaro Schoeck (www.charlottewaltert.com), which is based on Inglin's novella Die Furggel (translated in this volume as The Fork in the Valley) and his novel Die graue March (The Grey Borderlands).

Greylands was premiered at Animafest Zagreb in June 2023 and subsequently shown at various international festivals including Fantoche (Baden) and Imaginaria (Bari).

Chris Walton is an honorary professor at Africa Open Institute, Stellenbosch University, and currently runs two research projects for the Swiss National Science Foundation at the Bern Academy of the Arts. He was awarded the Max Geilinger Prize in 2009 for his contribution to cultural relations between Switzerland and the English-speaking world.

CONTENTS

Preface 1

Näzl and the Ragdoll 5

The Burial of an Umbrella-Mender 13

The Fork in the Valley 23

The Hedge 39

Meinrad Inglin with binoculars, 1963.
Photo: Helen Weber.

PREFACE

Meinrad Inglin was born on 28 July 1893 in Schwyz, the tiny capital city of the eponymous canton. His father, a goldsmith and city councillor, died in an accident in the Glarus Alps when Meinrad was just thirteen; his mother died four years later. Unsure of his future path, Inglin began then abandoned two apprenticeships, first as a watchmaker, then as a waiter. Subsequent enrolments at the universities of Neuchâtel, Geneva and Bern also proved of brief duration. Journalism became his doorway to a career as a writer. He was appointed to a part-time post with the *Berner Intelligenzblatt* in 1915, then to the editorship of the *Zürcher Volkszeitung* in 1919. But just half a year later he resigned, determined to become a freelance novelist, and returned to his native Schwyz to write. His first novel, *Die Welt in Ingoldau (The World in Ingoldau)*, was published in 1922 by the Deutsche Verlags-Anstalt. It established Inglin's name but caused a scandal in Schwyz, where many believed it to be a misanthropic depiction of their city. Inglin, however, always insisted that it was no *roman à clef*, but a more general depiction of a stale, arch-conservative, Catholic community. Schwyz and its environs remained a vital force throughout Inglin's oeuvre. This is true of his novels, including *Grand Hotel Excelsior* (1928), *Die graue March* (1935), *Schweizerspiegel* (1938) and the more openly autobiographical *Werner Amberg* (1949) and of many of his short stories, of which we offer four here in English translation for the first time. These are *Die Furggel (The Fork in the Valley)*, first published in the collection *Güldramont* in 1943, *Der Lebhag (The Hedge)*, first published in the yearbook *Die Ernte* in 1946, *Näzl und Wifeli (Näzl and the Ragdoll)* and *Begräbnis eines Schirmflickers (The Burial of an Umbrella-Mender)*, both of which appeared in the volume *Verhexte Welt (A World Bewitched)* in 1958.

Inglin married his longstanding partner Bettina Zweifel, a violinist, in 1939. During the Second World War he served in the Swiss Army as a lieutenant colonel and was for a while in charge of internee camps for French and Polish soldiers. The post-war years brought a series of major honours, including the Swiss Schiller Prize and an honorary doctorate from the University of Zurich, both in 1948, and the Gottfried Keller Prize in 1965. This late recognition was not, however, reflected in financial success, and he and his wife were for a long time largely dependent on her income as a violin teacher. Besides novels such as *Urwang* (1954) and *Erlenbüel* (1965), Inglin's later years also saw him publish a large number of short stories.

The four stories published here all thematise the individual in the landscapes of Central Switzerland. In *Näzl and the Ragdoll*, an isolated high alpine pasture is the setting for an eerie tale that takes up the old alpine legend of the 'Sennentuntschi' in which a cowherd lonely for a woman solves his problem by making one. *The Burial of an Umbrella-Mender* reveals Inglin's gift for comedy and his eye (and ear) for the quirks of village life. *The Fork in the Valley* is a late reworking of the mountain accident that killed Inglin's own father. And *The Hedge* shows a concern for the environment that was many years ahead of its time. In a seemingly simple story about a stubborn old farmer and his hedge, Inglin describes how man's heedless destruction of Nature wreaks havoc in turn – not just on those responsible, but on everyone around them and on subsequent generations.

Meinrad Inglin died in Schwyz on 4 December 1971. His archives are held today by the Schwyz Cantonal Library, and his collected works are published in ten volumes by Limmat Verlag, edited by Georg Schoeck.

Chris Walton, Solothurn & Törbel, Michaelmas 2023

Meinrad Inglin and a mountain panorama.

NÄZL AND THE RAGDOLL

He'd been baptised Ignatius thirty years before, but they all called him 'Näzl'. A farm labourer and a cowherd, he was ugly of feature and uncouth of nature, so no woman ever gave him a second glance. A bachelor with no wife to still his lust, he took instead to prowling around after dark, harrying the women and the girls about. On his last evening before driving the cattle up to their summer pasture on the alp, Näzl lay in wait for a girl at a farm outside the village, hoping she might emerge to fetch the washing hung out to dry behind her house. She was only seventeen, so if she wouldn't give him willingly what he wanted, he could easily take it by force. But she never came. He watched through the window as she snuffed out her bedside candle, and then all was silent save for the snorting of the livestock in the adjoining stable. So Näzl went round the back of her house, stole her undergarments from the line, and took them with him when he left early next morning for the mountain.

The alpine pasture lay high up between rough, craggy cliffs, and during the summer months it fed at best fifty cattle and a few milk cows. With nowhere for them to stray, the animals were easy to tend. Näzl also had a boy to help him – fifteen-year-old Karl, whom they called 'Kari' – so the life he led up there was hardly a harsh one. Kari had to make the fire, wash the dishes and feed their only pig. It was his job, too, to carry the butter down into the valley and bring back firewood from the forest. If Näzl didn't have to milk the cows or churn the butter, then he lazed in the sun and hungered for a woman.

One day, Näzl took out the clothes he had stolen and stuffed them with straw. When the boy came back from the meadow, he asked, laughing, 'Are you making a ragdoll?'

'Yes', said Näzl, 'that's what I'm doing.'

It was boring without any women around, so he'd make one himself. He used an old sack for a skirt, fashioned the head out of moss and rags, and cut slits in it to make its eyes, mouth and nose.

'That's a proper scarecrow!' cried Kari when the thing was finished.

It looked like one. But Näzl called it Dolly. He put his arm round its waist and danced with it.

In the evening when they sat down to eat, he called, 'Come here, Dolly, sit with us!' And he placed it on the bench by the wall, behind the table.

There it sat in the shadows, lit up only by the fire in the open hearth. But when a flame flickered high into the air, it looked almost alive. Once, it bowed slowly forwards before falling breast first onto the table. Kari laughed, but Näzl cried out that the girl was still weak and they'd have to feed her to get her strength up.

'Are you hungry?' he asked, and wiped some butter into its mouth.

As night fell, he said, 'Come, Dolly, it's time for bed.' He carried it up to where he slept and lay down next to it.

This he did for a few days. But the strange creature wasn't good enough for him anymore, so he made all kinds of improvements. A little butter helped, here and there. The next night, the doll seemed to sigh a little and warm itself against him. He sat up, startled, which in turn woke Kari on his straw bed.

'What is it?' he asked. He got no answer, though he saw how Näzl lit the lantern, shone it over his bed, then snuffed it out once more and lay back down.

The next day, Kari went down to the valley to deliver the

butter. He'd stay there till the next morning, then return with bread and other necessaries. Näzl did his rounds on the pasture towards evening, checked the state of the grass, then at last began to wonder whether it was really the ragdoll whom he had heard sighing in the night. It was impossible to believe. It must have been his own snoring that he had heard. But what if it *was* her?

He halted at the farthest edge of the pasture, by the mounds of rough boulders that had once dislodged themselves from the weather-beaten cliff face. And he stood there alone, brooding on it all. The evening was heavy with a coming storm and the cattle were grazing by the hut. Far and wide there was no other man but he, and in this eerie isolation he began to ponder things as might someone already half out of his wits. What if he could create a living woman for his own pleasure? A young, pretty, living woman? Damn it, if only! He thought of his ragdoll. He could now spend a night alone with her for the first ever time, and he felt drawn to her as to a real girl. He returned across the pasture as night was falling and the dull hammering of thunder echoed in the black-green twilight. He came to the hut, his gaze fixed. He went inside and took Dolly in his arms.

He sat her next to him at the table and whispered filth to her. He drank black coffee with schnapps, took her on his knee, dipped a finger in the alcohol, stuck it in the ragdoll's mouth and told her to suck. Finally, he carried her up the ladder and lay down with her on his bed. Once more she seemed to warm herself against him, and he could hear her begin to sigh. He thought it might just be the storm-winds hissing as they passed over the shingle roof. But he felt a fire raging within, and as two arms clasped themselves around him, he heard a voice that said, 'Stay by me, don't be afraid, I'm only a poor girl.' He gave a mighty start, and for a while was sure he had lost his senses. But he could not prise himself away, for his lust was stronger than reason.

Just before the first morning light, he crept out of the hut. It was raining, but he ran around barefoot in the meadow as if drunk. When daybreak came, it sobered him up. He headed back to his hut, telling himself he must have dreamt it all. But the door was open, smoke from a fire in the hearth was wafting out, and a girl came onto the threshold to call to him.

'Come and eat breakfast, Näzl, it's ready!' She was wearing Dolly's ragged clothes but was so sparklingly alive, so young, so beautiful and well-formed: the prettiest girl he could ever have imagined. He acted as if he knew nothing, asking who she was and where she was from. She answered, laughing, that he knew it well enough. She was Dolly, and there was nothing else to ask.

Once more he was seized by terror, but he went in and ate with her. She laughed, chatted, cast him loving glances and sat on his lap, and he warmed to her again. He could not gaze upon her enough, she pleased him so well, and since everything now happened so naturally, his resistance vanished.

Towards evening, Kari came back. He was surprised to find the girl there. Näzl said she was his fiancée. He'd asked her to come, and now she was here. In order to save her better dress, she was wearing the scarecrow's clothes while she worked. Her name was really Katry, but he would call her Dolly. Kari didn't mind, since there was now another pair of hands to help.

But Näzl was soon completely under the spell of the unholy creature, and they led a shameful life together. As the summer neared its end, Näzl spoke of driving the cattle down the mountain. But Dolly asked him to stay and let Kari do it instead. He couldn't, said Näzl. He had to go down with the milk cows and five of the meat cattle; that had all been agreed in advance. After that he would come back, and then together they would take the herd down to the lower pastures where the owners would fetch their cattle. Dolly said nothing, but she looked at him with the eyes of a prowling cat at night.

Not long after, Näzl took the cattle down into the valley to their owners so they could parade them before the dealers who had come to check them out before they went to market. Näzl met up with a few cattle herders who had come down from other isolated alpine pastures and who wanted to drink and make merry in the village. They knew him as a notorious failed philanderer and asked lewdly if he'd managed to survive up on the mountain without a woman. Was he still 'fasting?' they asked.

In other years he would have cursed them all to hell and walked off in a fury. But now was different. He mocked them, laughing, and replied: if they thought *he'd* been fasting, then compared to him they'd all be wasted away.

'Oho,' they cried, 'then it's your round! If there's any truth in it, buy us a quart, it'll be worth that much!'

'You couldn't drink as much as I'd have to buy you,' he answered, banging his fist on the table. 'Hey, Marie!' he shouted to the waitress, 'bring us half a gallon!'

This made them all the more inquisitive. They huddled together, drank to his health and asked if an old beggar woman or a flea-ridden vagabond girl had stumbled upon him, up on the mountain. He answered them with all manner of grand innuendo. The more they doubted him, the more lavishly he boasted.

Then they wandered merrily through the valley, from one tavern to the next, and not until around midnight did this raucous band set off noisily for their own village again. It was a stormy night. The full moon shone, jagged clouds scudded across the sky, and the mountain forests were alive with pale glimmerings and dark shadows. Näzl could hold his tongue no longer. He cried out that no one else had ever had a girl as pretty and as passionate as his, and whoever didn't believe him would see it for themselves soon enough. One of the drunken cowherds pointed at the nearby field and asked: 'Is she as pretty as that one?' In the middle of the field there stood an old scarecrow in a tatty grey skirt, with crooked arms and a head made of rags. Its right hand was held up high, and from it there dangled what looked like a black knitted bag, but was in fact a half-rotting crow that it seemed to be waving at them.

'Look, it's my sister-in-law!' cried Näzl. He jumped over the wooden gate into the field. He ran over to it in his drunken high spirits, took this ragged scarecrow in his open arms and began to dance with it.

The cowherds leaned on the gate, laughing and egging him on with their cries and cheers. But soon they wondered how anyone could dance like that over tilled earth. For before their eyes, the two figures spun round, each held tight to the other's breast like a couple on the polished dance floor of the tavern, only faster. It was uncanny, for it seemed as if Näzl was no longer dancing of his own free will. He was being whirled round and round, faster than even the lightest on his feet could manage. One by one, their drunkenness left them and they fell silent. Pale to a man, open-eyed and open-mouthed, the cowherds stepped back from the gate in horror at what they saw.

As the couple spun madly in a breathless flickering of moonbeam and shadow, a whirlwind went out from them, piping a howling dance and scattering soil from the field, setting the willows and alder bushes a-tremor down by the brook. Not a sound was heard from the dancers themselves. But Näzl's clothes fell from his body like old rags, his skin was shredded, his blood gushed out and around, and his raw flesh shrivelled away. When his flayed figure finally vanished from view, the whirlwind ceased, the scarecrow was again in its place, and the night was as before. The wind whistled through the valley and clouds scudded past the moon.

The cowherds walked back to the village, pale and silent, and in the morning returned to their huts up in the alpine pastures. When asked later about Näzl, they said only that he must have had an accident on his way back up the alp, falling somewhere he could not be found. What they had seen that night with their own eyes, they told to no one. In any case, there was none who would have believed it. But the day before they returned again from their pastures, one of them went up to help young Kari. He said that Näzl had gone into the valley with the cattle. The night after that, his girl had run off. He had seen nothing of them since.

Meinrad Inglin on a meadow near Leysin, 1963.

THE BURIAL OF AN UMBRELLA-MENDER

It was in Vorderau in the wintertime, when the snow lay thick about, that our two vagabonds first became acquainted. They had never met before, but immediately found each other's company so agreeable that they embarked on a meandering tour from one tavern to the next, downing schnapps as they went. They were both on their way to nearby Hinterau, but were drunk by the time they tottered out that evening. The snow scrunched underfoot as they left the village, making their way through the fields to Hinterau along a narrow footpath that was shorter and quicker than the road. The smarter of the two was a basket-weaver, a gaunt fellow in an old overcoat too big for him that hadn't always been his own. He found a little shed, its door unlocked. So he stopped, called to his friend, then went in, covered himself with straw and slept. But the other man, an umbrella-mender, was determined to reach Hinterau that same evening. He staggered on into the pine forest where all tracks ceased to be, and he now marked out his own path in the snow, grinding and hewing it with his feet as he went, though without wandering unduly from the footpath proper. After crossing the village boundary that cut through the woods, he tripped over a jutting tree root. He fell down, decided to rest there for just a moment, but then lay so snugly in the soft, fallen snow that he soon fell asleep. An ice-cold, crystalline January night now descended that no slumbering drunkard could survive out in the open.

The next morning, the basket-weaver left his shed and went on his way. He read his friend's footstep scrawls in the snow and smiled at their sweeping flourishes. Suddenly, however, he found the man lying before him, frozen beside a tree root. He couldn't be woken, and not even a half-hour of hefty pummelling could bring him back.

'Well, that's it', said the basket-weaver. He got up, sweating. 'You're done for, my friend. As I reckon, you lay down here at about nine last night and now it's eight in the morning. That makes eleven hours of sleep at fifteen to twenty degrees below zero. I'm sorry, but I can't help you anymore. All I can do is make sure you're buried as a good Christian with the blessing of the church. Yesterday, as I recall, you swore at the heavenly host like an old heathen. You won't get through the pearly gates as easily as you crossed this parish border here.' He slipped his friend's rucksack under his head, crossed the man's icy hands over his chest, and walked on.

He went to Hinterau and was soon in the company of three village councillors. They could have sent someone else to bring back the frozen umbrella-mender, but instead they wanted to come and see things for themselves. The gentlemen examined the corpse briefly, making evident their annoyance that a vagrant had been so inconsiderate as to freeze to death right here, on their land. It was bothersome, and burying him would be expensive. They huddled together to discuss the case, then looked up and glanced around. The ground here – they told the basket-weaver – really belonged to the neighbouring village, so it would be best if he went back there and told *them* of the misadventure. Then the people of Vorderau would see to the dead man.

The basket-weaver agreed with a blank face and wandered off a hundred paces towards the next parish. But then he left the path and swiftly turned back across the border. He had barely hidden himself behind a thicket of pine trees when he saw the gentleman councillors carrying the dead man past the border stone. He grinned as he watched the little funeral procession, but when the triumvirate returned a few minutes later, minus their unhappy burden, he strode out. Tapping the border stone with his hand, he addressed them in a friendly tone. 'Hang on there, please, just wait a moment!'

The astonished gentlemen conferred briefly, then came and stood around the vagabond. Their chairman took out a five-franc piece, toyed with it in his right hand, and explained, 'We merely helped him a little along the way to Vorderau. But we can bury him at our village too. It's up to you.'

'I don't really mind,' answered the basket-weaver. 'But in any case, he's now in Vorderau.'

'Precisely!' confirmed the chairman, pressing the silver coin into his palm. 'And you know nothing different! No one would believe you anyway, and we know nothing either. Now go along to Vorderau, and when everything's in order, come back to me at the Sternen tavern and you can have a proper supper and a pint of wine.'

After the deputation had fulfilled its task and was on its way home, the basket-weaver went back to his friend where he lay in the snow, next to the path, and pondered their situation. 'Five francs, a supper and a bottle of wine are what you're worth to them, no more. But now I want to know what you're worth to the Vorderau people. Whether you're buried there or here, you'll get your Christian burial!'

So he returned to Vorderau, bought a cheap sheet of writing paper and two different envelopes, went into the Sonne tavern, ate lunch in their warm front room, then asked where he might find the chairman of the village council. It turned out that it was the landlord of the Sonne itself.

'Excellent!' said the basket-weaver, and told him that his friend was lying, frozen to death, in the wood.

15

The chairman asked, 'Where is he, precisely?'

'On the Vorderau side, near the border stone,' answered the basket-weaver. 'He was drunk, and first wandered over the border to the next village, but then came back.'

'A pity!' said the chairman. 'As far as we're concerned, he could have stayed over there.'

The basket-weaver then pondered, 'If someone were to give him a hand, he'd soon be back there.'

'Do it for him!' said the chairman. 'Hinterau is a better-off village than ours, he'd get a much better burial over there. If you were his friend, you could surely do this last favour for him.'

'I don't really mind,' answered the basket-weaver. 'But since he's now in Vorderau, he'll probably have to be buried here. That's why I came and ate my lunch here. If I have to go back to Hinterau and spend the night there, I'll just have unnecessary costs.'

'It doesn't have to cost you anything, and you can even have your lunch on the house. In Hinterau you'll be able to get a nice room and have two meals for — let's say — ten francs. A good deed is worth as much to us, only it would have to be done before we could reward it.'

'I can see that, sir, and I'll try,' said the basket-weaver. 'I just need ink, a pen, a bit of sealing wax and a glass of wine.'

He got what he wanted. He had stuffed a paper serviette into his coat pocket while eating and now took it out, folded it differently from before, slipped it into one of the envelopes, and sealed it with the wax. After that, he wrote a letter, placed it above the tiled fireplace to let it dry, then put it together with the sealed envelope into the second, bigger, yellow envelope. He sealed this, too, wrote on it, allowed this also to dry on the heated tiles, and then returned with it to the forest.

He went back to his frozen comrade, who still lay on the Vorderau side, and said to him, 'You've gone up in value. You're worth ten francs now, but only if you're buried in Hinterau. So you'll have to come back with me over the border. I've got your pass here, and it'll probably help you to stay on the other side for good.' He opened the dead man's rucksack, hid the yellow envelope among its dirty clothes, then dragged the rigid corpse across the border. He laid him down in the snow and went on his way.

In Hinterau he went straight to the local priest and told him everything that had happened – omitting only the details of his own role in it all.

'The men from Vorderau,' he concluded, 'also didn't want to keep my poor, dead friend, but had him brought back to the Hinterau side where he'd been at first. I don't know what I should do now, it's already dark outside. I don't know anyone here, and if we don't bury him, the foxes will get to the body.'

The eager young priest was outraged at all these unworthy doings. 'Come with me!' he said, and thereupon went with the basket-weaver to the Sternen tavern, where the three councillors were sitting for their evening tipple.

'Mr Chairman, an awful thing has happened,' he began. 'Out there in the forest a man has frozen to death, a friend of this fellow here. Please see to it that he is brought here immediately.'

The chairman was also the landlord of the Sternen and a well-fed, broad-shouldered man. He rose ponderously and explained the situation. 'That's right, Father, but the dead man lies on the Vorderau side, and this fellow here had the job of telling them over there.'

'I did that, sir, but the Vorderau people didn't want him either,' said the basket-weaver.

'What, they didn't want him either? That's all we need.'

'Let's not argue!' cried the priest. 'It's my duty to take care of the departed. I'm going out there now and want you gentlemen to come with me!'

They argued for a while nonetheless, after which the chairman left with the priest, the basket-weaver and the councillor whose office of almoner put him in charge of poor relief. Out they wandered again into the forest, through the pale, snow-bedecked January night. The village gravedigger also came along, dragging a sledge behind him on the orders of the priest. The almoner went ahead with a lantern.

'He's right,' he called as they came upon the dead umbrella-mender, 'there he lies…'

'… again!' added the basket-weaver, loud enough for all to hear.

The chairman looked daggers at him and said, 'We should have brought the village policeman along – a pity he's not here. We're obviously dealing with people who can't read or write and who don't even know each other's names. Father, we're going to check here and now, in front of you, to see if this dead man has any papers on him to tell us who he was. And we'll see if he's still got everything on him that he had this morning. We don't want to be accused of anything after the fact.'

The almoner examined the dead man's belongings. In the rucksack, among the dirty washing that he had not deigned to touch that same morning, he found a sealed, yellow envelope.

'Here's something!' he cried, and read what was written on it. 'To be given to the priest of the parish in which I happen to die.'

The priest took the envelope and opened it. The gravedigger held his lantern high, and the men huddled together to read what was written on the sheet of paper that it contained.

'Mr Chairman', said the priest, taking a step backwards, 'I want to read this here and now, in front of you, so that everyone present can hear it and no one can reproach us afterwards.' And he read quietly, his voice trembling with emotion. 'In the event of my death, I hereby bequeath 500 francs and ask in return for a church burial in a proper graveyard. And the bell should be rung for me as it is for every Christian on his passing, and a mass should be read for my poor soul. All those who carry me to my last resting place should then be given ample food and drink. Whatever is left of the money should be put in the poor box. Here is a sealed envelope, with the money in banknotes. It has to be given to the priest and may only be opened on the day after my burial, so that nothing goes amiss. The chairman of the parish and two councillors are then to fetch it from him. This is my wish. God have mercy on my soul! Alexander Huser.'

The basket-weaver, who had expressed himself in curses while the letter was read, now called out, 'The crafty old fox! He said he didn't have a penny on him, and he had me pay for the schnapps he drank! That takes the biscuit!'

'Under these circumstances,' said the chairman, 'we'll have to have it announced in the police bulletin. It's dated... can I see that again, Father? It's dated as of two years ago, there's no place mentioned. And now let's see the envelope with the money...'

'Oh-oh!' cried the basket-weaver.

'Everything is in order,' declared the priest. He put the smaller sealed envelope, unopened, back in the yellow envelope along with the letter, placed this in his inside jacket pocket, then turned to the vagabond. 'I'll see to it that everything is done according to the wishes of your deceased friend and that nothing untoward happens. I promise you that. And now, let's put him on the sledge.'

The frozen umbrella-mender was loaded on the sledge, the almoner went ahead with the lantern, the gravedigger pulled the sledge, and the others followed in silence. Despite the late hour, there were still a few inquisitive folk in Hinterau who followed the sad cortège to the graveyard, where the body was laid out in the chapel.

The basket-weaver was given an attic room in the Sternen. The next day he was a guest of the house, and everyone could read the sadness on his face. While walking through the village, he came across an old woman collecting rags, along with a few other poor souls, and he urged them all to pay their last respects to his homeless friend the following day.

The next morning, two gravediggers carried the frozen umbrella-mender in his black coffin out of the chapel. The coffin was followed by the basket-weaver, who bore the wooden cross for the grave, the parish scribe with a pine wreath, the priest in his white robe, the sacristan, a delegation from the village council, and various members of the poor. The bell chimed solemnly through the cold, clear morning. The procession made its way to the nearby grave where the deceased was brought in dignity to eternal rest with the blessing of the church. The basket-weaver's tears ran down the stubble on his cheeks, and when at the end he sprinkled holy water onto the coffin in the open grave, he murmured, 'Cheers, you old rascal,' visibly moved.

The mourners attended the poor fellow's funeral mass in the village church, after which a meal was offered in the Sternen as requested in his last will and testament. The mood soon became more spirited, and the departed's friend was especially prominent among those eating and drinking. But the chairman of the council had no intention of having this errant tramp live and eat at his tavern's expense, so he didn't wait long before handing over the deceased's belongings to him, along with a reward of twenty francs.

The basket-weaver left the friendly village of Hinterau early the next morning without announcing his departure. He moved on to the neighbouring village, where he drew yet another bonus; he left Vorderau shortly thereafter. He regretted that he was not able to be there when the chairman of the Hinterau council opened the sealed envelope in the priest's house, but otherwise he was perfectly happy. He then vanished, never to be seen in either village again.

Meinrad Inglin on a rock face, early 1900s.

THE FORK IN THE VALLEY

A father and his twelve-year-old son were walking eastwards along the gentle incline of a valley in the grey light of an early September morning. A light mist hovered over the broad stream that flowed calmly past them, with alder bushes on the one bank and meadows full of herbs on the other. When their path took them close by the water, or across a wooden bridge to the opposite bank, the wanderers felt the mist gently caress their faces. Dark, wooded slopes loomed through the haze on both sides of the valley, which rose steeply towards the pale blue of the morning sky.

This was the first time that the boy had been allowed to accompany his father into the country where the hunting season for the chamois goats was now beginning. He had been waiting in blissful anticipation of everything that this long-desired day might bring with it. He could not yet keep up with the tall, strapping man beside him, though he would never have admitted that his father in any way shortened his stride for his sake, not even by a finger's breadth. He paced alongside the man in happy excitement. His youthful features already revealed early, well-defined hallmarks of his father's face. Full of curiosity, he peered about on all sides and listened keenly to his father's every word, following his gestures with rapid glances. They came to a short, level patch, at which his father began to whistle a march tune and took slightly shorter steps so that the boy, striding out, could walk in time with him. The next ascent on their path brought the whistling to a close, at which each of them fell back into his own walking rhythm. As they did so, they looked at each other and laughed; they were good friends.

They soon reached the foot of a hillcrest covered in trees where the valley forked into two: the stream became two brooks, while their trail divided into a narrow road on the one side of the mountain and a footpath on the other. As they took the latter, which led up the narrower, steeper valley to the south-east, the father pointed towards the edge of the forest where a boulder lay that was the size of a man, overgrown with ivy, moss and ferns.

'It was from this green escarpment,' he said, 'that I shot the big fox whose fur your mother now wears. It weighed eighteen pounds.'

'That's a lot, isn't it?'

'Yes, really a lot. Normally, foxes round here weigh about twelve to fourteen pounds when they're fully grown.'

'But isn't a fine pelt more important than what he weighs?'

'That's right! And this mountain fox already had his lovely, long, winter coat. That's why your mother got him. He was loveliest, of course, when he was still alive, wandering the woods or hurrying out of the dark pine forest, silent and keen, running between the bare beech trees, his coat shining a lovely reddish yellow in the sun.'

'Yes, I'm sure… But I'd have shot him too.'

The father laughed. 'You see! Many people don't understand that you can get the greatest pleasure from living creatures out in the wild, and yet still hunt them. That's a contradiction, they say. Well, it might be, but life has many contradictions. We can't resolve them all, and yet life is still beautiful.'

All the while, they ascended briskly up the steep path, then halted on a narrow bridge to take in the fresh breeze that shadowed the course of the tumbling waters. They looked down into the main valley where the stream took its zigzag course westwards, enshrouded in the mists that they had left far behind them. It was their last sight of the valley, for their path now took them along a shadowy mountain slope that hardly afforded any view at all. But sometimes, between the pinnacles of the pines, they saw a long cliff rising up to the south of them. The father pointed to it and said, 'When we're up there, we'll see the alpine pasture, and behind it lies the ridge of the *Furggel* where we're heading.'

'Why's it called that?'

'Because of its shape. The *Furggel* is elsewhere called *Furkel* or *Furka* – it's an old word meaning "fork", and simply means a place in the mountains where the land splits into two…'

He broke off, turning his attention instead to the path further up ahead. Above the murmuring of the little stream, they could hear dogs barking, cowbells, and the 'hoi, hoi' of the cowherd driving his cows from the alpine pasture down into the valley. A young girl emerged first and walked shyly past them, followed by about thirty cows and yearlings, of which several gazed inquisitively at the two wanderers as they moved aside and halted to let them pass.

The father went up to one of the cows, and with his fingers stroked its wrinkled forehead from one horn to the other. 'That's a *Furggel* too,' he said, 'that's the shape of it.'

The cow was pressed onwards by the one behind it. The one after that plodded wilfully out of line and began to munch at some grass, as if it were all on its own. But a black-and-white sheepdog ran up from behind, barking to drive it back onto the path. Finally, the bearded cowherd arrived, a pitchfork on his back and a silver-studded pipe in the corner of his mouth. He was accompanied by a man with a rifle.

'The one with the gun is the gamekeeper,' explained the father swiftly to his son, then greeted both of them. They all knew each other, and their faces brightened as they stopped to chat. The cowherd knew full well why the father and son were out here, and began without prompting to tell them of the mountain goats he'd seen that summer – some on the *Furggel*, some farther away on the meadows with the limestone outcrops. The father asked about their number, how many rams there were, when they'd been to a certain salt lick, and about the numbers of a different herd. The cowherd answered as well as he could – or at least as well as he wanted. The gamekeeper listened to all this without saying a word himself, then the father asked him if he knew someone who might help out in the coming hunting season.

As the man pondered it, the father said, 'Perhaps you'll think of someone. I'll call on you on the way back in the afternoon, it's on my way. You can count on it!'

The cowherd and the gamekeeper shook his hand in parting before walking briskly after the cows. The father and son climbed higher up the hill. They soon reached the edge of the forest where the sky was blue and cloudless. Beneath them ran the path, little stony hillocks on either side as it curved and narrowed, threading its way between cliffs that suddenly opened up towards the east. From here they had an unexpected view of the green alpine pasture, drenched in light and surrounded by higher mountains on all sides. Father and son stood silent. The sun glistened before them. All was quiet.

The boy gazed in happy astonishment at this mighty, serene highland world. He looked at his father, who nodded cheerfully; then he looked out on it again, and breathed a sigh of deep contentment.

After a while they reached a broad, smooth meadow.

'The saddle of the mountain over there is the *Furggel*,' said the father, 'that's where the cowherd saw the goats.'

'Do you think we'll see them too?'

26

'It's possible, if they're still there. But a cowherd doesn't always know things so precisely. The gamekeeper could have told us more.'

'Why didn't you ask him?'

'Precisely because he's the gamekeeper. He keeps an eye on the wild goats here the whole year round, protecting them from poachers. He knows them and is fond of them. I could have asked for more information and perhaps he'd have told me – he's a decent fellow and we understand each other well. But I want to spare him that – he shouldn't have to tell me where I can shoot the animals he tends to. In the hunting grounds it's different. There, the gamekeeper is employed by the hunters and tells them what he knows. But here, hunting is still open to everyone; so here, the hunter himself has to keep his eyes and ears open if he's to find his quarry.'

They wandered across the empty pasture, climbing up and along the eastern incline towards the broad ridge of the *Furggel* between the mountaintops. Sometimes they halted, and the father peered through binoculars at the distant slopes. When they finally arrived at the *Furggel*, they crept quietly along on hands and knees across the loose, gravelly rocks and the sparse patches of grass until they reached the other side of the ridge. Here they lay watching, and the boy's eyes glistened in expectation as they scrutinised the distant scene. But they saw no goats.

They stood up, and only now did the boy realise that yet another, new mountain world lay before them in the east: a world of which he had noticed nothing at all along the way. His father explained that this was also typical of a *Furggel*.

'In our Alps, there are other such landscapes that go by this name or something like it. Sometimes they correspond to a border, and they almost always signify a pass through the mountains. They are also often a watershed where the rain drains down into the valley. The best-known, and one of the biggest, is the Furka Pass. Mountain climbers know these *Furggel* as well as they know the mountains themselves. You walk and climb and you sweat, then as your reward you stand on the pass, with your path behind you and a new world before you. You also get it in life. It's like a mountain hike. There'll be a few times when you stand at a fork in the valley like a *Furggel*, dividing your path into two – like on exam days at school, at your wedding or when someone dies. But enough of this. Let's eat something now!'

They found a comfortable spot and sat next to their rucksacks. While they ate bread and cheese, the father listed the names of the mountains that they could see. Then he said, 'You'll have to wait for me here. The path gets more difficult over there, with places where you have to climb steep rocks. I've promised your mother not to take you there. You'd manage it – you're skilful enough, and you're not scared of heights. But I've given my word. It suits me, too, if you stay here, because then you can tell me if any goats move over to the broad ridge on our left. That could take two or three hours if they come at all, depending on where I find them. You don't need to pay any particular attention – but if you happen to hear any little stones trickling down from there, stay quite still and take note. Otherwise, you can do whatever takes your fancy while you're here. You could go over the ridge up there on the right if you want, but don't go too far down – and watch out for the rocks, because some of them are razor-sharp on their edges. Or you can go back to the ridge where the sun is shining. You might see some marmots, for they have their lairs there. And if I'm not back around midday, then eat something. I'll take something with me to eat, just in case, but I'll leave the rucksacks here.'

He nodded to the boy as he would to a friend who knew his innermost thoughts and intentions, then went along the ridge where the northern summit rose up sharply. There, keeping to the right, he climbed over a sloping scree of rocky debris leading to a band of grassland that lay to the north, on the steep eastern edge of the summit. He turned to his son, who had followed him as far as the scree, nodded to him once more, then strode out along the precipice as if he were traversing a secure bridge. He now disappeared from sight.

Here, the grass had still been cut. But farther on, where the pasture became ever steeper, no reaper would have space to swing his scythe, so the grass lay long, thick and smooth on the slanted patches, hanging over the edge of the void like tousled horses' manes. The father went carefully around the slope, grasping tufts of it with both hands in order to steady himself until he saw the broad, old rocky ridge that he wished to reach in order to begin his descent. On its green, overgrown middle hillock, he espied some goats. He huddled on the ridge and reached for his binoculars, as a hunter does, without thinking, but as he did so he slipped and plummeted silently down, still with clumps of grass in his fists.

In the meantime, the boy stood on the edge of the *Furggel* and gazed out at the world before him, near and far, in high spirits, like a young prince who has inherited his father's realm and lords over it from his lonely throne. Towards the east, the *Furggel* dropped down onto a slate-grey, time-eroded slope that led into a broad hollow full of rocky debris. This led in its turn to a bright green, terraced alpine pasture that formed dark green hills in the distance. Above them, a chain of snow-covered peaks glistened in the blue of the sky. To the right, the long expanse of the alpine pasture was bordered by white-grey, shimmering limestone outcrops, while to the left it sloped down to the forest's edge. If you looked past the dark tops of the firs, you would see the yawning abyss of a distant valley with steep banks of trees rising up beyond it towards brown patches of wild grass and a range of hills at the same altitude as the *Furggel*, where the cows went to pasture and the grass shone green against the shock of blue sky.

The boy looked at all this and gazed insatiably about him, time and again. He found it magnificent beyond words to be standing up here, in the midst of this tremendous world, looking upon it as if it belonged to him and him alone. He walked along both sides of the ridge, then returned to the sunny side where he found the entrance to a marmot's subterranean lair. After looking closely at it, he lay behind a little hillock and waited with immense patience to see if one of the nutbrown bundles of fur would truly try to slip out. When he tired of this, he went over the ridge towards the limestone outcrops and looked in wonderment upon the naked array of rocks that the ice of ages had groined, filed and barbed to razor-sharpness.

Around midday, the boy returned to where the rucksacks stood, ate a little, then lay down and observed the broad ridge below the eastern summit, for this was the hour when the goats might move along it. He watched intently for a long time, to be sure that nothing escaped his attention, but then became sleepy. He closed his eyes now and then, but made sure to listen carefully. He was sure that he would hear if any little stones trickled down to signal the approach of the wild goats.

Half awake, half dreaming, he felt the sun cross his face as it wandered to the west. The light on both rock and grass became warm and golden. He now slept a little, and thought he saw his father return over the gravelly slope. He half-awoke again, and realised that he had been dreaming.

Then he woke with a jolt, lifted his head and looked around him with surprise. The warm light was extinguished and the world looked quite different. He stood up, rubbed his eyes and surveyed the scene. The sun had gone down. The mountains all stood against the dark, quiet blue of the evening sky, unutterably calm and clear. But the nearby cliffs, limestone ridges and meadows lay lacklustre and colourless, as if shadows had wafted across them.

He stood for a long time, barely moving, and only then did his real wait begin. He had not been aware of 'waiting' before, but now this was all he did. He waited for his father, and wanted nothing else.

Evening came, the blue light faded from the sky and the alpine meadows below him sank into the twilight. All at once it turned cool, as if the warmth of day had been brushed away. Night fell, darkness began enveloping everything and the blue-black arch of the firmament began to glitter.

The boy went to the scree and peered into the distance, unceasingly listening and waiting. It seemed to him as if the quietness was becoming ever quieter, the heavens above him ever farther away, the earth ever less visible. His sense of daytime majesty had given way to a mood no less intense, but which was now dominated by feelings of insignificance and abandonment.

It became ever colder as night encroached. It was September, and at this altitude, the next break in the weather could bring snowstorms as heavy as in winter. The boy was not dressed warmly, for he was supposed to have been back home with his father long before now, not still waiting for his return. He felt the onset of frost and began walking to and fro on the ridge to warm himself. Once, he halted in his movements, and stared over at the scree. His heart beat faster, and expectation robbed him of his breath. Something was moving on it: a small, grey figure hurrying towards him, growing to the size of a man as it came, but then it billowed outwards and was only the head of a thick, grey, snakelike trail of mist. He felt betrayed and angry – not because of the mist itself, that would have been foolish – but because he had let his sense of expectation delude him. He turned away, frowning, and spotted yet another band of mist that snaked its way up from the depths of the valley, rising high up into the gathering twilight. While he gazed on, it rose close towards him like thick smoke, swiftly and noiselessly encircling him. He stood in the grey-black darkness and saw nothing more, and since he knew how easy it is to lose one's way after just a few steps in the mist, how easy it is to lose one's sense of direction, he remained where he was. From time to time he called out, more confident than frightened, as you might cry out in the forest to a companion you'd only just seen: 'Hallo!' His voice was bright and firm and hadn't broken yet. But it seemed to him that the darkness swallowed up his cries the moment he uttered them. So he called even louder.

After a while – he was unsure how long – the mist suddenly dissolved, allowing him to see the starry sky clearly. Then it welled up again, halted for a while, and yielded once more. This was nothing unusual in the autumn; it happened in the mountains by day and night. But this enduringly indifferent, ghostly, inconclusive to-ing and fro-ing chilled the lonely waiting boy to his soul. Another while passed, and an unseen force pushed the mists back down to the valley. Now the clear alpine sky itself began to frighten him. The rocky limestone wastelands shimmered pale below, the white snow-capped peaks hovered as a phantasmal apparition in the twilight, the valley depths yawned black below, and while the sky glistened close and bright, its stars were inconsolably distant. The more time passed, the more sinister everything seemed to the boy, sowing the seeds of despair in his anxious heart. He called out no longer, for it was pointless. After a while, he cried out meekly, with a gentle reproach in his voice like a child afraid of the dark, 'Father!'

Sometime between midnight and dawn, the booming cries of a strange, rough voice startled him. He immediately heard the scrunching steps of someone approaching from the western face of the *Furggel*. He listened and called back 'Hallo!'

The man answered in turn and was soon standing beside him.

It was the gamekeeper. He looked at the boy, looked around the ridge, and asked, 'Where's your father?'

The boy told him.

The gamekeeper was silent for a moment, then said, 'Well... wait here! Two men are coming up, tell them I said they should wait here for me.' He paused and seemed to ponder something. 'Your mother was asking about you down in the valley,' he explained calmly, with a nod of his head towards the boy. 'Well, I'll go and look now.' With that, he finished speaking, and strode over the rocky scree to the band of grass where the boy's father had disappeared from his sight that morning. The gamekeeper lit the lantern that he had brought with him, and then he too fell away from view, along with his swaying light.

He soon returned, extinguished his lamp, but did not come up to the ridge, descending instead to the rocky debris. He skidded down, the stones grating underfoot as they yielded to him. Then his steps became firmer, but they receded from earshot as he went farther away along the foot of the mountain face.

The early grey light of morning was just emerging over the snow-capped peaks when another man called out from the western pasture. The boy called back, though his voice now almost failed him. Two men came up. One of them was the cowherd who had taken his cattle down into the valley the day before. They listened to what the boy said, nodded, and waited.

By the time the gamekeeper returned, the mountains in the east shone golden in the rising sun. He came over the scree to the two men, and they huddled together to talk. The boy took a few steps toward them and saw how the three of them whispered to each other. They peered at him, conferring with muffled voices, and he stood there until they at last approached him. His knees trembled.

'It would be best if you went home now,' said the gamekeeper. 'You can go back with him there.' He nodded towards the cowherd. 'He's got to go down too... you share the same path.'

The boy's throat seized up. He stared silently at the gamekeeper, but then went slowly over to the two other men. He stood motionless between them and looked at no one any more.

The cowherd told him to come home now, and the gamekeeper spoke to him too. But he simply turned away.

The men conferred again, then the cowherd left without the boy, hurrying swiftly down towards the alpine meadow.

The gamekeeper said, 'If you want to stay here... I can't stop you, but it would be better if you went home now. Your mother's waiting for you... we've got to go back down there.'

The boy couldn't utter a word. He just stood and gazed into the emptiness with wide open eyes. But after the two men had descended onto the scree once more, he turned to follow them.

The gamekeeper heard him and waited for him at the foot of the eastern face. 'You can't come with us!' he exclaimed.

'It's much better for you if you don't come with us.' Since the boy stood there silent and motionless, he put his arm around his shoulder and spoke on, softly. 'You have to pull yourself together and be sensible! You're not a child any more. And try and bear it, for God's sake, there's nothing can be done now.'

The boy pulled away from the man's arm and turned his back to him. Terrible agony ravaged his face, and tears streamed from his eyes.

'Leave us!' said the gamekeeper. 'Think of your mother, she needs you now and is waiting for you. Farewell!' He walked away, slowly, along the wall of the cliff.

The boy knew now what had happened but could not comprehend it. He felt as if he were held fast in a giant, clenched fist that shook him to and fro. He couldn't move away. Slowly, he sank down, there where he stood, and remained on the ground, bent double, barely able to breathe for sobbing. The gamekeeper saw it, shook his head, and turned back out of sympathy. But when the boy saw someone coming to him, he quickly got up, an expression of defiance on his pain-rent face, and walked back up the scree.

When he reached the *Furggel* he went to the rucksacks, swung both over his shoulders – first the smaller one, then the large one that held their cooking utensils and their food, and which hung down to his legs. He climbed down the western face, crying all the time, went across the deserted alpine meadow and came to the narrow path with the cliffs on either side, now lit up before him like a golden gateway. Yesterday at this same hour, he had seen this mighty mountain world open up to him. He looked back one more time. The sun shone in his eyes, he saw the *Furggel*, and he turned away, shaken, sobbing bitterly.

He walked down into the forest and reached the place where they had come across the herd and his father had spoken with the two men. Then he came to the narrow bridge over the rushing stream where they had looked down into the valley for the last time to see how the brook wound its way to the west under thin swathes of mist. He recognised everything, but now he was alone. He looked in bitterness through his tears, and strode on.

But when he reached the green, overgrown escarpment at the edge of the forest from where his father had shot the big fox, he was overcome once more. An aching cry emerged half-stifled from his throat, and shook him to the core. It came upon him again on the short, level path where his father had whistled a march, where they had walked in step, and where they had laughed and revelled in each other's company. It rose violently within him after every anxious breath, surging over him like the intangible dangers of a dream, choking him in body and soul. But this was a waking terror that he had to bear.

He still did not halt on his path, and soon saw the little farming village in front of him, the same that they had left at dawn the day before. At the entrance to the village, he met the cowherd, who was already on his way to somewhere else, a hod over his shoulder, but held up in conversation with a bunch of men who were idling there.

The cowherd came over to speak to him. 'We've sent news to your home,' he said quietly.

The boy did not stop, but walked on, his head held high, already armouring himself with dismissive, headstrong defiance. The people moved silently to one side and looked at him. As he walked between the few huts and houses, he met other villagers. They looked on in sympathy as he came, grimly uncommunicative, his face tear-stained, two rucksacks on his back. The landlady of the guesthouse came out. He and his father had spent the night there, and now she called out to him: he could walk on home if he wished, but for God's sake he should rather come inside and wait a little. Yet he looked neither right nor left. He walked on hurriedly into the valley, his taut face pained and sullen, his tearful gaze focused on what lay ahead. He strode on into the next, bigger village, straight to his mother who was waiting for him. He poured his violent anguish into her deep sorrow, as after a thunderstorm the torrents of the mountain stream gush into the dark, mighty currents of the river, leading them on to a distant, greater goal.

Meinrad Inglin with garden shears, 1954?

THE HEDGE

High up on an open, sparsely wooded plateau, the farmers tore out all the hedges bar one, enclosing their fields and meadows instead with inanimate wire fences strung along iron posts. It was much more convenient and far safer, they said. A fence blocked no light from the soil and made no work for anyone. The farmers seemed not to care that the land now looked so bare, for their concern was only the use of it, not its beauty. After all, they were farmers.

The last green hedge owed its life to old Bonifaz. He was determined to preserve it, and each year took it on himself to prune back its mighty growth with his shears. His son Blasius, nicknamed Blaesi, would have gladly replaced it with a wire fence long ago, and only reluctantly indulged his obstinate father. Their land was a rectangle of which the western half was pasture, while the eastern half was partly tilled. Between these two halves stood their brown, two-storey wooden house, which merged as one with their barn and stable. The hedge formed the border of their land with a neighbour's pasture on the long, northern side. This neighbour had also suggested replacing the hedge with a wire fence, though he never insisted. He kept quiet out of respect for old Bonifaz, whose shears kept it trimmed on both sides.

It was a thick, full hedge of hawthorn, field maple, dogwood and other such bushes, intertwined with bear-bind and hops, and with flowers and animals sheltering under it. A proper, living hedge as a hedge should be. When the cut grass had been gathered on the meadow and the crops harvested, old Bonifaz would spend an unhurried day in the autumn sunshine, from early to late, traversing the length of his hedge.

He smoked sparingly on a lidded pipe that hung down into his grey beard. His bald, sunburnt head shone, and he gazed in friendly manner at the thicket before him, for he knew each and every shrub in it. Thorn saplings, leafy branchlets and tall switches fell from his mighty shears as he worked, calm and imperturbable. Often birds would flee from him, emerging from the thicket only to enter it again further along its length, and he would mutter at them reassuringly. A hare jumped out and away past his feet. He looked on, laughing, as it fled with raised ears, only to disappear in its hollow amongst the foliage. Sometimes a few hazel twigs would suddenly begin to dance before him and move away along the hedge. 'Upon my soul!' he would cry, 'the hedge is running away from me!' He would run after them, rattling his shears, until the chuckling behind the hedge turned to squeals of delight as his grandchildren jumped out at him.

These children, a boy and two girls, were allowed to play across the whole meadow whenever it had been mown or the animals had finished grazing on it. But they preferred to play along the hedge, hiding in it, discovering things in it, or just ambling in its shadow on hot, summer days. The hedge was their paradise and always remained so, even when they were old enough to go to school. Only there could they find the year's first primroses, wood anemones and violets, nowhere else. A little later, the hawthorn would begin to blossom, and it looked as if snowflakes had settled for good on the shorn, green hedge. At that time of year, the hedge began sprouting out everywhere, and Grandfather Bonifaz would show the children how the places he had cut short and bare were now teeming with new shoots. He led them gingerly to a bird's nest, trusting them to ensure it came to no harm. On one occasion, they in turn showed him a nest – a round, firm ball made of green moss with a single hole in it where the wrens slipped in and out. In May, Grandfather collected the tips of the thin, raw hops that already hung high over the hedge, and cooked them in a little pan with some butter until they were tender to eat. Between the thorns there blossomed privet, honeysuckle and woodbine, and in summer the spirea, columbine and other flowers would bloom along the side of the hedge – flowers that you never saw out on the meadow. By August, the hedge was so tall that a grown man could not see over it. And by October, when the sky was a deep blue, the falling leaves of many hues of brown made the hedge glow as if it harboured in it all the colours of the autumn. Many living things still found in it a final place of refuge and protection, both animals and plants. They remained hidden and unseen, though old Bonifaz knew they were there, and it pleased him.

One wet, cold autumn, Grandfather Bonifaz took to his sick bed, and stayed there for a long time. Neither his son nor his neighbour had the time or inclination to trim the hedge themselves, so they decided they would cut it down. They went to work in the winter, hacking and cursing and toiling away for many days. The hedge with its thick, knotted roots had a tenacious hold on life, and gave them more work than if they had taken turns pruning it ten winters long. The children looked on sadly.

'It's such a shame!' said the older girl, but her father told her it was high time to have done with that wild old thing, along with the weeds and the vermin that lived in it.

When the grandfather finally emerged the next summer and went out walking with his stick, he saw instead of his thriving hedge just a single iron fence. He said no word of it, but looked for a long time, seemingly unable to comprehend. He had only just reawakened to the felicities of life, but now all joy slipped away again as he stood and stared. The cheer of his old age seemed extinguished, its place taken by melancholy and frailty.

'The illness has had its way with him,' said his family. They never thought that an old man of lifelong habits might have any other cause to be disgruntled for so long.

It was the children who missed the hedge the most. Since it had gone, they never rushed back happily from school, for what had drawn them home so quickly was now no longer there. They still played in their free time, but boredom set in sooner than had ever been the case when they could enjoy the hedge with its inexhaustible delights. Their grandfather had nothing more to show them, and he no longer found much reason to spend time with them at all. As is the way with children, they didn't bemoan their hedge for long, and finally forgot about it. But the violent destruction of their paradise had eaten away a little of their exuberance, and this little, being so precious a thing, was something that they would miss in future. They did not realise it themselves, but they weren't as happy as they had been before.

The hedge had always been home to many birds: tomtits, robins, wrens and sometimes even chiffchaffs. They had fed off bugs, devouring more of them than a farmer would ever imagine might exist on his land. Now the birds were gone and did not come again, having instead found other shelter in copse and spinney. The little pests fared all the better – the kind that a man's eye only notices when they begin to wreak damage. Snout beetles multiplied, for their young could now spend the winter in the trees without danger. On the potato field, a beetle that had barely been noticed before gained the upper hand. Weevils, caterpillars, grubs and maggots of all kinds prospered unhindered. Throughout the year, Blaesi was perplexed first by this and then by that, by half-gnawed blossoms, leaf-eaten branches, blighted potato plants and worm-infested fruit. But this was only the beginning, for the vermin increased with every year, the harvest dwindled, and his frustration grew ever greater.

Hedgehogs living in the hedge had eaten cockchafer grubs and crickets on their nocturnal forays. But with nowhere now to hide in daytime, the hedgehogs moved away to seek other shelter. A family of weasels did the same after they were driven from their home in the hedge. These sleek, lean predators had hunted field mice year in, year out, following them relentlessly into their burrows. Now the mice bred rapidly and soon became a plague.

Blaesi could not understand all this. He'd never been much of a thinker, doing only more or less what he saw his neighbours do. He was at heart a harmless, pleasant-natured fellow, but now he was almost always in a bad mood. His family suffered under it. The other farmers had all endured the same, and so were not surprised to find Blaesi sharing their common woes.

Then there came a dry, windy year. Everyone swore things had never been as bad as this, not even in past years when the dry, windy spells had lasted even longer. God's bounty had disappeared from the land, they said. And yet that land was now open, sunny earth, tilled and cultivated to the last hand's breadth of it and divided up by clean, iron fences. In earlier times, the many hedges had fended off the dry winds, keeping the soil moist, and in weeks when it hadn't rained, there had at least been the dew to wet the earth at night. Now the wind moved over the land as if it were a bare, open steppe, and the few fruit trees were unable to hinder it. It damaged the grass, which grows unwillingly in wind. It dried up the dew and took from the earth the warmth and moisture it needed. It whisked up soil from the dried-out fields, blowing away the minerals from the surface that the meadow grass needs to help it grow. This happened during the worst of the cold, windy season. But it also happened in the dry weeks of summer, if less perceptibly. The old, fertile earth slowly became barren.

This and other evils would have each been bearable on their own. They would have caused no cries of protest, and the farmers would have hunted out their cause. But together, they were hard to bear. Blaesi was convinced that there must be something deeply wrong, for how else could he explain that from one year to the next his blossoms, leaves and fruit were ruined by insects, that mice devoured everything everywhere, and that the crops no longer grew thick and upright in the fields, nor the grass on the meadow?

Yet this was only the damage that could be seen and measured. Blaesi and his family now suffered another loss that was incalculable and far more difficult to recognise. It had begun when old Bonifaz, who had once kept all their spirits high, descended into melancholy, triggering frustration in turn among the children. The gradual diminishment of their happiness seemed negligible at first, but it was a happiness that they could have stored up and drawn upon to their benefit in later life. Blaesi's annoyance at his run of bad luck compounded everything. He was in a constant foul mood, which also made things bad for his wife. Joy had deserted them.

The other farmers began using machines and artificial fertilisers, and they sprayed poison to kill the insects. Blaesi watched them do it for a while, but ultimately decided it was pointless and a waste of money. Besides, everything had gone so much better in previous years, and they'd never used anything artificial back then. He didn't think it worth his while to exert himself unduly, and began to neglect all manner of things.

'It's as though it's jinxed. Nothing's of any use!' he cried. And because he couldn't bear it, he sought forgetfulness by getting drunk on cider and schnapps.

The elder daughter got married as soon as possible. The younger couldn't stand life at home much longer, so moved out and took a job as a maid in a good house, which pleased her more. The son's only role model was his moody father, so he too lost all pleasure in farming. One day he disappeared, only to write from far away that he was working in a factory. He was sorry, but at least his new job wouldn't work him to death. He would also earn a proper wage and got time off.

Blaesi got drunk that day. When his wife reproached him, he complained that it wasn't his fault that everything had gone wrong: the Lord had taken His blessing from them, and he didn't know why. His wife was an austere, hard-working woman, but no cleverer than he.

'Then we'll have to pray for His blessing and go more often to church,' she replied. She was perfectly serious, and since Blaesi had remained a religious man through everything, he did not contradict her.

Prayer and churchgoing helped the pair of them to overcome their deepest discouragement for a while. But it didn't help their crops. Once man loses his sense of the wonder and beauty of Nature, he acts less according to Nature's wisdom and more of his own accord, ignoring or misusing what God has granted him. Even if he went to pray for help in all the churches of the world, it would still be in vain.

Blaesi continued to drink. His wife often had to see to everything on her own. One morning, after he had sobered up, he came to the breakfast table in a hideous mood. His wife complained bitterly, he swore at her, and they began to argue loudly. She couldn't stand it anymore, burst into tears, and turned in desperation to her old father-in-law. It couldn't go on like this, she cried, she just didn't know what to do any more.

Grandfather Bonifaz sat at the table, weak with old age, trembling as he dipped bread in his milky coffee. But he now awakened from his lethargy, listened for a while, then said in his quiet, rough voice, 'You've got to tear out the wire fences and plant green hedgerows. Then it will all gradually get better.'

Blaesi and his wife couldn't grasp that this might be their problem, and thought the old man's advice fatuous. They laboured on until he died, then they sold their run-down homestead and moved away. They didn't have the sense to understand that Bonifaz, with the simple wisdom of experience and old age, had told them the truth. Nor did the other farmers of the region have any more sense than they. The time wasn't ripe for it.

It might seem strange that an act so negligible as uprooting a hedge, an act now so long forgotten, should have brought such desolation to so many. But it is hardly strange that something as fragile and tenuous as human happiness might be struck down by something that seems just as slight. The frost needs only to loosen a few stones on a cliff for a boulder to tumble down. A teardrop can suffice to tilt the golden scales awry. In the life of country people, it can be something else – a valley floor sold off and flooded for a hydroelectric dam, a forest torn down that no one had ever realised was essential, or a lovely grove of trees whose value is unwittingly measured out in money alone. Here, it was a hedge.